D0821016

M**O**THER

load

ALSO BY AVERY CASWELL

LUCK, A Collection of Facts, Fiction, Incantations & Verse

MOTHER load

stories by
Avery Caswell

LORIMER PRESS
2015

LORIMER PRESS
First Edition

ISBN 978-0-9897885-7-1
Library of Congress Control Number 2015936863

Printed in the USA

COPYRIGHT © Avery Caswell 2015

All rights reserved. In accordance with the US Copyright Act of 1976, reproducing any part of this book without the permission of the publisher is prohibited. To use material from this book (other than for review purposes), written permission must be obtained from the publisher.

This is a work of fiction. Any similarity to real persons, living or dead, is coincidental and not intended by the author.

Cover art based on an illustration by Arthur Sarnoff, courtesy of Heritage Auctions, www.HA.com

For Kurt

CONTENTS

"Parenting is something that happens
mostly while you're thinking of something else."

— Barbara Kingsolver
Quality Time

FOR YEARS I BELIEVED my brother and I were Irish twins. But when I mentioned this to my college roommate, Meghan O'Donahue, I discovered I had been misinformed. Meghan set me straight. The actual definition of Irish twins is siblings born in the same year (and, FYI, is an ethnic slur against the Irish, so I hesitate to even mention it here). My brother Matt and I were *not* born in the same year, but on the same day, two years apart. (March 3rd: third month, third day, making "3" my lucky number.) I like to think we had a bond like real twins—that we had some secret connection. We did and we didn't. We did when my brother wanted to.

We certainly didn't share a secret twin language, but to the never-ending dismay of our mother, we delighted in off-color jokes. We both liked black licorice and hated ketchup. And for our birthday, instead of cake we always asked for a big bag of malted milk balls. He made a point of giving me odd, non-girly gifts—one year a blow torch, another a butterfly knife with a hefty six-inch blade that is probably illegal in most states.

This year, there will be no gift from my brother. I am celebrating my birthday alone, trying and failing not to feel sorry for myself.

You're thinking surely some friends will call the poor girl and invite her to dinner or at least a drink. Where are her friends anyway? Is she so socially inept that she has none? Well now, let's think about where we meet most of our friends: At work. With our significant others. In our neighborhoods.

Those realities no longer apply to me. It's embarrassing to explain that I was fired. Humiliating to say my boyfriend preferred my best friend. I have nothing to say to my so-called former friends. I plan to make some new ones. Once I get everything under control. Currently, I have some issues that make acquiring friends a challenge.

I'm more than a little rank.

Thrilled as I am to have a roof over my head, I'd kill for a shower. A shower and a laundromat within walking distance. Jeans are great until it comes to washing them, and worse, getting them dry. Somehow turning a hair dryer on them, even at full blast, does not accomplish that fresh-from-the-dryer smell. Plus, wearing damp jeans in late winter can leave your thighs chapped.

Humid, fabric softener-scented air is being vented into the hall this afternoon. I can only guess it's coming from a clothes dryer at Scissors, the beauty shop in this complex where I am sitting at my drawing table in dank, putrid smelling jeans, obsessing over the scent of Downy.

I should investigate the dryer situation. Maybe I can work a deal. What kind of illustration would hair stylists want to trade in exchange for laundry room access?

Probably none.

Two weeks ago, I sold my car and with the proceeds rented a key man office here at Heritage Plaza, a sweet little complex with awning-covered shops in front: a hair salon, dress shop and restaurant, each with pansy-filled concrete planters flanking their doors. Behind these hide a dozen, very plain 12 x 12 offices. Number 108 now serves as both my personal and business address. The rent is lower than a legitimate apartment. There's a bathroom down the hall. No shower, but I'm pretending I'm on a vacation—in Europe, an Italian *pensione*—rinsing my undies in the sink every night.

I'm learning the rhythm of the place. Traffic is slow at Scissors before 9 AM; Monkees, the dress shop, does not open until 10, and Bennett's not until lunch. The back halls, this warren of key man offices that I now call home, come to life first. The accountant in #105 is always here first, precisely at 8 AM. If people still wore watches, they could set them by her comings and goings. She goes to the ladies room at 8:05, then the break room at 8:10, where she puts on a pot of coffee (which I hope is communal; as soon as I am more financially flush, I'll contribute to the coffee fund, I promise). She tucks her lunch in the refrigerator, usually a pimiento cheese sandwich and a piece of fruit. Her little brown bag always goes in the fridge, even if the fruit of the day is a banana and brown by noon. At noon, she eats her lunch and rinses the coffee pot. There are two guys who may be appraisers or in insurance or investments. I'm not sure. Both look pretty nondescript, though one is taller and completely bald, the other short and paunchy. They usually go to lunch together at Bennett's, stopping in the parking lot before and after for a smoke. Both leave between five and six. A marketing professional rolls in around 9:30, aflutter in fancy blouses and expensive suits. She spends most of her time on the phone with her door open and I can't help but overhear the important media deals she is brokering. (I can't help but hope she has multiple clients with illustrative needs and I strain to hear the details.) There is also a husband and wife team who conduct geological surveys. Rounding out the group of tenants is a sales rep for some kind of technical equipment company who seems a little shy and a lot goofy, but is always pleasant when our paths cross at the drinking fountain.

Why all this surveillance? I'm trying to blend in. The last thing I need is for the building manager to discover that I am calling 144 square feet of this office building home.

I've half expected my mother to call all day; maybe I should call her, spill my tale of woe at her feet: *Yes, Mom, I've lost my job, my boyfriend and the roof over my head.* The very day I got fired from my (horrible) job designing parade floats, I went home to discover my boyfriend in the shower with my best friend. There is no describing the physical pain—as if a knife were turning, not in my heart, but my gut. It is still difficult to think of anything but Ty. Ty with Ashton. Ty with her *and not me.*

What will my mother say? *I'm so sorry dear. I always thought Tyler was such a nice boy.* I dial her number, a landline at her house in the Mennonite community to which she has returned. It rings seven times. Mennonites do not believe in answering machines. At least they have phone lines. On the eighth ring, she answers.

"Hi Mom. It's me, Marann."

"Well hi, honey. This is a surprise. How are you?"

"It's my birthday, Mom."

"No, it can't be." She sounds confused. Then alarmed. "Are you sure?" I can hear the gears locking into place. If it's my birthday, then it's Matt's birthday.

A quick change of topic is in order. "Guess what? I've opened my own design studio."

"What?"

I tell her a little about my plans and she asks, "What does Tyler think about this?"

"We're taking a break."

"What does that mean? Did he break up with you?"

"No, Mom. Not really."

"But I thought you two were getting married."

"No, Mom."

"If you need to come home—get your head sorted—there would be a place for you here."

"But what would I do there, Mom?"

"Peter Schmidt recently lost his wife."

That hangs in the air. I realize most men my age in the community are long married. My only hope now would be unfortunate widowers like Mr. Schmidt.

"There is always work for willing hands, Marann."

"I'm an artist, Mom."

"You could set aside time for making pictures."

"Good to know I have choices."

"Think about it, Marann." There is a little pause while we both scramble for something else to say. She thinks of something first. "Isn't twenty-six the cutoff for being on your parents' health insurance? You'll have to take care of that now."

Right, except I'm twenty-seven.

She has a point though. I haven't done anything since being fired. I make a mental note to subtract even more from my non-existent income. "Thanks, Mom."

"Good luck with your enterprise, Marann. Work hard."

"Thanks, Mom. I will."

Later, when I hear some of my neighbors packing up for the day, I think at the very least I could treat myself to a dinner at Bennett's. One more little charge on my MasterCard won't hurt. Too much.

Bennett's has been in this little plaza for as long as I can remember. Tyler never wanted to eat here. Not even for lunch. When it came to sandwiches, he said Bennett's depended more on mayonnaise than meat and served a chicken salad more onion than mayo. It would do for my "Hooray! I have a roof over my head" birthday dinner. And it's an easy walk home. The restaurant occupies the southeast corner of the plaza, opposite the salon. Inside, Bennett's is dimly lit, filled with standard issue Mediterranean. The small bar to the left of the door features amber glass divider panels and black wrought iron bar stools. The restaurant is crowded and the hostess is fielding several requests. The smell of steaks grilling nearly brings me to my knees. I can't remember the last time I've eaten red meat. Or white meat. Or any meat-like substance. Reading the menu, perched on an easel by the door, I discover Bennett's has hired a chef of some renown, one who uses heirloom tomatoes and signature greens and eschewed mayo in favor of herbed aioli. Bennett's is now expensive.

"How many?" the hostess asks. "None," I answer. It's easier than saying table for one, being seated next to the kitchen, suffering the embarrassment of ordering the cheapest thing on the menu and running the risk my credit card will be declined.

I walk back toward my office, trying to convince myself that I'm really not hungry anyway. As I pass the concrete planters in front of the beauty shop, I pick a handful of pansies and push them to my nose. The scent reminds me of my brother, or more precisely his nasal spray.

Matt had been so allergic to pollen that every day, from our birthday until spring was done blooming, he had to take a daily dose of nasal spray and a little white pill. He never minded the pill but hated the spray. Said it smelled like pansy stems. Despite his allergies, his sense of smell was far more acute than mine and he would have made a good perfumier. Growing up, we played for hours filling empty hotel shampoo bottles with our own concoctions—potions we called them—a little hand cream, shower gel, some toothpaste, whatever we could find that was scented. Playing potions with me was about the only thing my brother did that didn't involve risk. Matt loved anything that got him moving fast and preferably not in a straight line—roller blades, trick bike, skateboard—he mastered them all.

Matt. Our dad had predicted his last words would be "Hey, watch this." Damn. Maybe they had been. I don't know.

When the call came from Brazil, it destroyed my mother. They said he'd fallen. Maybe he'd fallen. Maybe he'd been pushed. Maybe he'd jumped. But his body was somewhere halfway down a mountain in the National Park *Serra dos Órgãos*, with its virgin forest and fantastic waterfalls. Officially, he was: Missing, Presumed Dead.

My mother, shrouded in her fog of grief, had moved back to her childhood home in Walnut Creek, where she no longer fully acknowledged or experienced much of anything. It had been nearly a year. Long enough for the shock to wear off but not nearly long enough to fill the void. For my mother it looked as if no amount of time would be enough. But anyway, *Happy Birthday, bro*. I salute him with a handful of pansies.

As sweet as the pansies smelled, their delicate fragrance is no match for Bennett's steaks. No matter what I try to tell myself, I am hungry. I have to eat.

Across the street from Heritage Plaza is a Handy Pantry where, "THIS WEEK ONLY!" is a "2 FOR 99¢ BURRITO SPECIAL"—if not perfect, at least an affordable birthday dinner.

The Pantry is a clearing house for local needs and wants. Taped to the door today is a piece of paper with a picture of a cat, a little calico with a sweet face. The bottom of the handmade sign is torn into vertical strips, each with the same phone number hand-printed on them.

MISSING CAT
"RAMBO"

last seen on
Feb. 27th
Please Call or Text!!

"Who could name a little kitten like that Rambo?" I ask, heading toward the refrigerated cases in the back.

Sylvia, who usually works the evening shift, says, "Tell me about it. Any one with a lick of common sense knows calicos are female and you can't name a girl Rambo."

"The cat probably left home on general principle," I say and set my two burritos on the counter.

"I just hope the poor thing's found a home. Feels like death warmed over out there."

"I know. I'm ready for spring."

"Who isn't? You oughta get some of them chips and salsa to go with your burritos. Salsa's on special, too. Less than two bucks for that movie star kind."

"Oh, just the burritos." But it's my birthday and I need dessert so I add a package of Hershey's Whoppers. "And these."

Sylvia is mid-thirties, a no-nonsense kind of woman who, if I had to guess, drives a solid, American-made sedan, always pays her rent on time and never forgets to roll her bin to the curb on trash day. Her oxford shirt, with "Sylvia" on the left breast pocket, embroidered in swirly italics with the word MANAGER in solid sans serif caps below, is freshly ironed. So are her khaki pants, the pleats crisp over her pelvic bones. She is just the left side of pretty—it's not as if she doesn't try. She's wearing lipstick, but it's a shade of red that makes her teeth look yellow. Her brown hair is scraped back in a severe ponytail with a brisk row of bangs that hangs a half inch above her eyebrows. Her starchy efficiency makes me feel even more unkempt, more pathetic. How is that even possible?

The counter is cluttered with point-of-purchase options, including a cardboard display of five-hour energy vials, the kind truckers like. Next to that is a big jar of change with another homemade sign. This one says, "Help Joan's Kids!" and features a picture of a heavy woman with stringy hair and an oxygen tube disappearing into her nostrils.

"The cancer got her," Sylvia says. "Was in her lungs, but it spread. All in her bones, now. That's two twenty-five with tax."

I hand Sylvia my last three dollars; she hands me back three quarters. I hesitate, but only for a second, and drop them in the jar. Three. My lucky number. Maybe they'll bring a little luck to Joan's children.

"Two little ones, just five and six," Sylvia says. "Ain't right. Makes me mad at God."

Me, too.

I eat one of the burritos on my way back to the office. The other one I consume in the hall. I like the quiet hallway of Heritage Plaza Office Suites after hours. It seems to be happy for my companionship at this time of day when the place is usually deserted.

A note is stuck to my door.

What a mood killer. I close the door. Lean against it, slide to the floor. Sing a little vintage Aerosmith.

Let me tell you what I think about *my* sit-u-a-tion... Complication? Aggravation?

MARCH RENT
PAST DUE !
—MGMT

They don't even come close.

Steven Tyler wears a necklace with four raccoon teeth. It's for luck, he says.

My father had a stone with the number seven worn into it. He carried it every day. For luck. Until he dropped dead of a heart attack when he was only 47. So, seven was not his lucky number after all. After the funeral, Matt slipped the rock into his pocket.

Sitting on the floor, my back to the door, the weight of my reality is more than I can bear. My credit cards are maxed out. I have exactly zero dollars and zero cents in my pocket. Instead of planning my wedding, I am plotting how to live undetected in a windowless box. I've been here for two weeks and haven't drummed up a single client. I stink. And my own mother doesn't even know how old I am.

I lean over until my head is on the floor and I am positioned like the girl on the proverbial railroad tracks. Instead of the roar of a locomotive, the thump of a radio playing somewhere in the building vibrates against my ear. Petroleum-based carpet fibers burn my nostrils; the smell fights with the sour odor of my poorly washed clothes. My cheek, raw from rivers of silent tears I cannot stop, burns too. My gut, not entirely happy after two cheap, bean-filled burritos, seizes and I curl into a ball.

I really thought I could turn things around. I've searched high and low for another job. I hoped once I had a place to live—stopped couch surfing, stopped sleeping in my car—things would turn around. So I sold my car and rented this office. I've been here two weeks trying to find clients. One client. Any client. Nothing's better. It's worse.

It could be over just like that.

Maybe this is how my brother felt toward the end.

I cannot hurl myself off a mountainside, or off the roof of this building, as its single story might fail to produce even a broken bone. Without a vehicle I cannot asphyxiate myself by inhaling carbon monoxide. No matter, all I need is a knife. Not my x-acto blade, as I'm in no mood for delicate incisions, but the butterfly knife, which is engineered with precision and better suited for a desperate gash of defeat. It can be opened with one hand by simply releasing a latch and swinging the knife open. In the Philippines, they call these knives balisongs—a lyrical name for such deadly steel. Matt told me this one was especially durable because the blade was made from old railroad tracks. The hilt is carved from water buffalo horn. So I'm certain it's up to the task.

One pull is all it would take. Here along my wrist.

I grip the hilt in my right hand and at first the metal feels cool against my skin; as it warms, I turn it over. Should I clean it first? As if that mattered. This isn't surgery. Cause of death will not be infection for crying out loud.

Will I have to slit both wrists or will one do? One will be all I can stand. So if one is not fatal, sterilization *is* necessary.

I hold the blade over my wrist for an hour, maybe longer. Paralyzed, I see no way out. I see no rosy future. I have no job, no income, only debt. There is no love on my horizon. All that has been offered me is Peter Schmidt, Mennonite widower.

How much blood will there be? Will it spurt out and stain the ceiling and walls or will it just pool on Heritage Plaza's carpet?

Now I know why people do this in bathtubs.

Oh just hurry up and get it over with.

Who will find me? Who will even think to look? No one. I will rot here until the stench alerts someone, probably the punctual accountant.

If I have to do both wrists, it will require greater strength to make the second cut, so better to begin by using my non-dominant hand. I transfer the knife to my left hand. I turn it so I see only the edge. This is where I am poised, right on the edge of a knife and the blade is paper thin. I could so easily lose my balance. On either side is an abyss.

I have two alternatives: Falling into the unknown, or striding like a tightrope walker to the hilt.

The blade glistens. Tantalizes me. Is it begging me to stay right here teetering on its edge? I cling to the reality of the pain slicing through my entire being, through the soles of my feet and into the core of who I am. A failure at everything.

What do I have to lose?

Nothing. I've already lost everything. Except—

I can hear my brother's voice. *C'mon Marann, you didn't* **lose** *anything —your job, your boyfriend, the roof over your head—you know where everything is.*

And I think, Peter Schmidt did not lose his wife, he knows exactly where she's buried. And Joan's kids aren't *losing* their mother either.

But maybe Matt *is* lost.

Lost like Rambo.

But what if the cat doesn't consider herself lost? It's possible she just set out to find a new life.

Maybe my brother has, too.

Maybe I should.

I'm 27—my lucky number, to the third power.

THIS IS NOT ADVICE for rank amateurs. Becoming a great son takes years of planning. Don't fall into the trap of last minute rebellious behavior, or the ill-conceived notion of doing the opposite of what your mother tells you. Don't fall for cliché concepts like being a picky eater, ignoring curfew, or dating women she'll hate.

Instead, begin early. In your toddler years, master many skills, but under no circumstances let your mother catch you: A. walking, B. talking, or C. tying your shoes. By all means learn these things and learn them early, but do not deprive your mother of the joy of doing them for you. She loves carrying you everywhere, coaxing you to say a few words and bending over to tie your shoes.

As you grow, exercise your intelligence. When you're off to school, finely hone your memorization skills and apply this talent for total recall by reciting scenes from R-rated movies and singing songs by obscure rappers on the playground. (And there's an additional benefit: You and your mom can spend more time together when the principal sends you home.)

As you progress through elementary school, repeatedly score in the 98th percentile on national standardized tests and consistently bring home Cs or lower on your report cards. In middle school, when you find yourself faced with a term paper, throw yourself into the research and writing. Ask your mother to proofread your humble efforts, knowing she will be blown away by your deep knowledge of all three phases of the Peloponnesian War and how it reshaped modern-day Greece. Draw parallels between the warring cities' distrust of each other and the woeful economic straits the country finds itself in now.

Months later, when you are failing World History, let your mother find this stellar term paper, un-graded, crumpled in the bottom of your back pack. This thoughtful gesture will free her from the obligation of ever attending another Parent/Teacher conference where all she's ever heard is: "Your son is very smart, but fails to apply himself."

Never underestimate logic. When your mother asks, "How in the world could you forget to hand in your term paper?" say: "You know, Mom, I think I accomplished the real objective. I learned all about the Athenians and the Spartans and that Pericles was killed by the plague, not by his enemies. Isn't it kind of a waste of time *proving* what I know when I should be moving on and learning more cool stuff?" Put your arm around her shoulder and give her a little hug. Then rap the Gettysburg Address and the Preamble to the Constitution in their entirety. She will be speechless, thus leaving you able to pursue more serious endeavors like perfecting a 50-50 grind on your skateboard.

Always try to get home *before* curfew; the earlier the better. Sit with your mom and watch the ten o'clock news. When you hear her sigh over the latest crime wave or voting scandal, ask her: "What do you think would solve the problem?" Listen thoughtfully to her answer. Then say: "Mom, you should run for city council." When she says, "I could never mount a winning political campaign," offer to write her a campaign rap. She'll laugh and call it a night.

Wait until she has fallen asleep, secure in the knowledge that you are safely home, before heading back out to the real parties. By all means, use the fire escape ladder that hooks right on your window sill, the one she bought after you showed her the fire safety pamphlet they passed out at school. It would be a shame if that purchase were never used, a waste of her hard-earned money.

Be generous, even from an early age. In second grade, when you have a hankering for a honey bun, don't be selfish. Demonstrate your generosity and declare to the entire cafeteria, "Honey buns for everyone—on me!"

Your mother will be happy to pay the $79.80 that appears on your school account. Trust me, she will be touched by your big heart.

Carry this personality trait forward; continue to make her proud by always being a great host. When you have people over, break out the best stuff for your friends, especially that case of sparkling Vouvray. And for non-wine drinkers, share that 21-year-old bottle of Glenlivit. It's older than you are! What is your mom saving this stuff for anyway?

I cannot over-emphasize the importance of developing a great sense of humor. Declare yourself the King of April Fool's jokes. Begin with tooth-paste-filled Oreos and graduate to slipping dead, soft-shell crabs under your mother's pillow. Serve her liver paté made from your dog's ALPO as an appetizer with her glass of Chardonnay. End your reign at age 20 by arranging for campus police to call her in the early morning hours of April 1st. Have them ask her to please come and get you. Immediately. The greatest zinger here is it will be *real*. This one she'll never forget. (And again she'll get to enjoy more quality time with you now that you're expelled.)

Always be kind and considerate and you will have "great son" written all over you. Be the only member of your family to notice when your mother gets her hair done. Tell her she looks great. And mean it.

Offer to run small errands for her, like mailing date-sensitive documents when you see she is juggling multiple deadlines. It's a given that you use her car for these short trips around town, as college dropouts have a hard time affording transportation and all. Be sure to take a more round-about way to the post office so you can pick up a friend. Impress him by demonstrating the speed of your mom's new car on an unfinished street with exposed manhole covers. Rip out the transmission, but keep going so you wreck the engine, too. Leave a solid trail of oil and underbody parts so you can find the abandoned car later. Lock the car to ensure the date-sensitive material that you were entrusted with is safely transported to the garage when you call a tow truck later.

By way of apologizing for totaling her car, set up a Facebook page for your mother and teach her about social media. Later, change her language setting to Pirate because, let's face it, your mom seems kind of depressed lately and you feel the need to lighten the atmosphere.

Repay your mother for all the trips she made to the Emergency Room when you were growing up and drive her there when she trips over your skateboard and breaks her jaw. Don't leave her bedside except when the doctor on call arrives. Take him aside and let him know that she is allergic to morphine. Suggest a phenylpiperidine or phenylheptane opioid such as fentanyl. (The doctor may raise his eyebrows, but your mom will be in too much pain to wonder how you know about all these prescription painkillers.)

And when your mother's hair begins falling out in large, unsightly hunks due to stress-related *alopecia areata*, find a wig with just the right blonde highlights. Remember, you're the only one in the family who ever bothered to notice when she used to get her hair done. She'll love you for it.

CHANNEL 18 INTERVIEWED HIM for the ten o'clock news. "The front window exploded," he said into the microphone, "and well, it was jes' kinda like the roof had a mind of its own. 'Sayonara,' it said. 'I'm outta here.' And *wham!* it was gone."

What he didn't tell the reporter was how he'd sat afterwards, covered in shattered glass, wondering *why* his roof up and left. Up and left like his ex-wife and his children and even his dog—up and left. All of them. As if being blown to bits and crash landing who knows where was better than staying with him. Was he such a poor excuse for a human being that, given the choice, everyone, and everything, chose to go?

That couldn't be it; he was the victim here. The victim of bad choices. He'd chosen the wrong woman, dog, dwelling.

Hadn't his mama warned him against Tina Marie, that hussy he'd married?

He heard that big shot of a politician from Texas saying how if he were elected president, he'd axe nearly every government department including and especially FEMA. "People are doggone fools if they choose to live in a flood plain or Tornado Alley. It's not the gov'mint's job to bail out the idiots who made bad choices."

Bad choices. That's what it all came down to. Choices. Good or bad. Take right now for instance. He could choose to light up this Camel and drink the last PBR before he drove over to the 7-Eleven to buy more of each. Or he could choose to wait. Or he could choose to change his mama's oil because she kept saying it was the least he could do seeing as how he was staying at her place rent free. Or, he could get up off this old, sprung couch and drive away.

Leave, just like the roof.

He'd just start driving and land who knows where. Start all over. Find himself a better woman, someone with a name that didn't sound like trailer trash, like Jennifer or Alicia. He'd move into a nicer place, maybe a condo, one with a pool. Hell, he could even get himself a new dog, one who'd jump on his lap and lick his face and wag his tail so hard he'd just about turn inside out.

He might. Once that FEMA check arrived. He just might. But right now he was gonna smoke that Camel and drain that PBR because by damn, he deserved it. After all he'd been through. Shoot—was still going through. Having to live with his mama. There wasn't enough beer and cigarettes in the whole world to make up for that misery.

He stuffed the still smoldering butt down the long neck of the bottle. Heard it spit and sizzle as it hit the bottom. Smelled the sour acid odor of yeast and nicotine and spat out the screen door.

THERE WASN'T A LOT TO DO before noon on a Sunday in Colonial Acres because everyone (respectable) was still at church. Usually the Dugans were too, but not this week because Frances's dad had a headache and Frances's mom wasn't about to go without her husband and so they didn't go at all. Plus they had to stay inside until noon because Frances's mom didn't want the neighbors to see them *not* at church. This meant no bike riding or walking their poodle Fifi.

One year shy of the nation's bicentennial, everything seemed to bear a patriotic theme—from frozen Red, White & Blueberry Waffles to hairstyles that involved a great deal of facial hair (Frances's father had grown sideburns) to real estate. In Colonial Acres, streets had vague ties to early American history with names like Davidson Drive and Pinckney Lane, after southern Revolutionary War heroes. As further evidence of where the developer's sympathies lay there was no Lincoln Avenue, but there was a Plantation Court and that's where Frances and her family lived in a gray split-level with white shutters and an attached garage. The drive was paved, not gravel; the backyard fenced, not with chain link, but with stockade. (And not a stockade fence like Harold Turner built when he came back from Vietnam with one leg. His fence was eight feet tall and surrounded both his front and back yard. He'd painted both sides black. Frances's mother said no one in his right mind would do that to a stockade fence.) The Dugan's fence was slowly weathering to a nice silvery gray. There was a gate between two sections of the fence and to the left of the gate was a playhouse with five windows, a door and a small stoop made of bricks left over from when Frances's father relaid the patio. The defining feature in the front yard was the iron

64 WITH A SHARPENER

jockey posted at the walk, his livery matching the house, his once black face now painted apricot. The jockey held an iron ring in one hand and from this hung a light, a light that much to her mother's dismay never worked because the rubber that encased the wiring had split in the heat.

Few of the streets in the neighborhood went very far; most dissolved into mahogany-colored mounds of clay, waiting for more families to succumb to the siren of the suburbs where monster machines with bulky shovels the color of goldenrod would move the red mounds to make room for another split-level, ranch, or if the newcomers had a little more money, a true Colonial four over four with a finished basement.

The development had once been farmland and sometimes a horseshoe or a bit of crockery could be discovered if there were nothing to do but dig in the dirt. A distant field was yet untouched. In its very center a live oak stood as if ruling the upstart colony on its fringes. Its branches, perfectly formed and evenly spaced, reminded Frances of a Joan Walsh Anglund drawing. Ignoring her mother's warning to never leave the neighborhood, last week, over spring break, when her mother was at some all-day meeting for new teachers, Frances had packed her crayons, a tablet of paper, two peanut butter sandwiches and a tiny box of raisins and headed for the tree.

The tree was farther away than it seemed.

The streets beyond her neighborhood were just dirt tracks. To reach the field, Frances had to walk along one of them and pass shacks that were barely the size of her playhouse. Her next door neighbor, Rhonda Ottman, had told her the people who lived there were all hiding out from the police. She said they stole food and swiped lumber from new houses and burned the wood to stay warm in the winter. Frances walked fast past these sorry little houses, afraid someone might jump out and demand her sandwiches and raisins, or worse, take her brand new box of 64 Crayolas with the built-in sharpener. She'd paid for the crayons herself with money her grandma had sent as a reward for another all A report card and she wasn't ready to part with them, not even for a starving criminal.

The field, long unplowed, was filled with rocky clumps of dried earth and half-dead weeds and not suited for ten-year-old girls wearing thin-soled Keds. It was even less suited to picnics. Bees swarmed when Frances opened her box of raisins. She threw the raisins as far away as her arm could muster, redirecting the bees, and then sat undisturbed, drawing and thinking how much better things looked from a distance.

— • —

Because the decision to not attend church this morning had been made at the last minute, Frances and her sister Lyndsey were still dressed in their matching Sunday dresses: Frances's was brown and black plaid and Lyndsey's, several sizes smaller, was blue and black. It was always this way. Lyndsey wore blue to match her eyes and Frances wore brown, a boy color to go with her boy name (every year the teacher read her name from the boys' list: Frances Dugan, right after Bobbie Cardwell) and her stupid, short, boy hair and boring, brown eyes. Frances had wanted the light green and blue dress but her mother said, "Green and blue? They don't go together at all." Whatever their color, the dresses were stiff and scratchy. Designed to look like jumpers, they had white collars and sleeves sewn into the neck and armholes, but Frances doubted that JCPenney's had fooled anyone. Her dress felt like it was lined with straight pins. The only good thing about this dress was that her little sister's had to be just as uncomfortable.

Frances and Lyndsey dawdled at the breakfast table while their parents read the paper. Lyndsey played with the remains of her scrambled eggs and Frances set up her box of crayons with the built-in sharpener. She knew it was time to move on to colored pencils—she was turning 11 next month —but pencils didn't have colors like melon or periwinkle or sea green. She liked the organization within the dusky yellow box, how the crayons stood at attention, separated into four compartments, two rows of eight each, the rows graduating in height like the risers she stood on in choir. She sometimes thought of the little boxes like voices: sopranos, altos, tenors and basses. She loved how even dull colors like carnation pink (which was too pale) and tan (which didn't really have much to say at all) looked prettier when they stood next to violet blue or aquamarine. Sometimes Frances didn't color at all, she just re-arranged the eight rows into pleasing combinations. When she did color, she was careful to rotate the crayons as she worked so she didn't blunt the tips. She had yet to use the sharpener in the back of the box; somehow it seemed wrong to subject the soft wax of her crayons to the blade.

When Frances opened the box today, her stomach clenched. There was a hole. One of the tenors was missing. Which one?

"Lilacs, Jim," her mother said from behind the paper, "I need some lilacs." She pronounced the word *ly-lahks* making the word sound so lovely that it distracted Frances for a moment from her missing crayon.

"Lilacs just don't do well here," her father said. He said *lie-lacks.*

Frances thought *ly-lahks* sounded better and she decided to always say it like her mother. *Ly-lahks, ly-lahks, ly-lahks* she murmured to herself, committing the word to memory.

"Why? I thought every living thing flourished in this humidity."

"I'm sorry Jess, but it just gets too hot for lilacs."

"It's too hot for everything *I* like." Jessica Dugan folded the Garden Section with a snap.

"What about crape myrtles? They're nice. There's a new shade of lavender at the nursery. It would be almost like lilacs."

"No it wouldn't." Her mother poured another cup of coffee.

Frances thought her mother could be a little nicer, especially since her father had a headache. Most of her parents' disagreements came about because her mother was someone who believed cold weather was a good thing and that jockey statues shouldn't be black any more.

"Crape myrtles don't bloom in May," her mother said. "I want something lavender blooming then."

Was lavender still in the box? Frances usually filled the tenor section with blues and purples. Plum? Red violet, mulberry? Yes. She lined all the blues along the edge of her placemat. Midnight, cadet, navy. Where was sky? Sky blue was gone. She looked under the table. On her hands and knees, she found a cold clump of mushy eggs and a bright blue hair tie that belonged to her sister.

Her mother pulled Local News from the stack of newspaper on the floor. "It says here, Jim, come fall, kindergartners are going to have to ride on a crowded bus for an hour-plus ride, twice a day."

"Bus sounds better than walking."

"I can't believe you want Lyndsey riding a bus for two hours every day."

Fifi, happy for company down on the floor, wandered over and licked Frances's nose, then ate the eggs. There were no crayons down there.

"But Jim," her mother said, "imagine what my classroom will be like if this new bussing plan gets approved. I'll have kids who are ready to read Shakespeare and others who won't even be able to pronounce his name."

Frances's mother crossed her legs, and from under the table Frances and the dog watched as she kicked one foot over and over, the toe of her high heel pointing straight to the ceiling, a sure sign her mother was not happy. The dog prepared to pounce, but Frances put her hand on its collar and shook her head.

Frances tugged on her sister's ankle, jiggling her foot so the dog jumped at it instead. "Lyndsey, did you take one of my crayons?"

Fifi, ready to play, gave a short bark.

"Frances," her mother said, "get out from under the table. Your sister did not take your crayon."

"But sky blue is missing."

"I think the dog got it," Lyndsey said.

Frances knew that hadn't happened. She never closed the box until she had every crayon lined up properly. She didn't lose it; someone took it. Stole her sky blue crayon. Probably her sister. It was a *blue* crayon after all and Lyndsey thought she had a right to anything that matched her eyes.

Or, Frances had a sinking feeling that it might be under the oak tree, in the field where she'd gone last Friday. Somewhere she wasn't supposed to have even been. Her stomach hurt even worse and her neck felt sweaty, which made the brown dress even more unbearable. "Can I go for a bike ride?" she asked her mother. "It's nearly twelve. People will be getting home from church now."

"Where?"

"Just around the neighborhood."

"I'd prefer you not play at the Ottmans' today."

Frances knew why. The last time her mother drove the carpool Rhonda Ottman had climbed into the Dugan's Volkswagen and announced that the boil on her butt had just popped. The seat of Rhonda's pants had been stuffed with toilet paper.

Frances's mother never said much during those short drives to school, but she communicated loud and clear via the rear view mirror with arch looks aimed at Frances and her little sister in the backseat. Dugans didn't get boils; they never said butt; they didn't even *write* the words "toilet paper" on the grocery list. Frances knew her mother thought Rhonda was a bad influence even without knowing that every day during morning recess Rhonda snuck across the street to Lawson's Quik Stop to buy chip-chop ham and cheese puffs so she didn't have to eat the cafeteria lunch.

As for the Ottmans' being off limits, it didn't matter because lately every time Frances went over there, Rhonda was at the Kings' house. Bambi King had moved from Atlanta after Christmas. Bambi King was now the prettiest girl in the fifth grade; and she would be, Frances knew, the coolest girl next year in middle school. She had long, dark blonde hair, dishwater blonde Frances's mother called it. It was a combination of maize with a little sepia mixed in. She wore it loose with a center part like Pocahontas. She met Frances, looked her up and down and said, "You don't look like a Francie to me, not with that hair. I believe I'll call you Frank."

Frances had worked hard during the first semester of fifth grade to get everyone to call her Francie, like Barbie's cuter, cooler friend. Francie, kind of a blonde version of "That Girl." Girls named Francie had best friends and boyfriends and fluttery lashes and always wore the right clothes in colors that were not brown. People named Frances didn't. After Bambi King moved to Colonial Acres, Francie was history.

"So can I go?" Frances asked her mother again.

"*May* I—?"

"May I go? Please."

"You need to change first."

Frances lost no time stuffing the bristly fake jumper in the laundry basket. She pulled on some shorts and a t-shirt. Her Keds were getting too small so she strapped on last summer's sandals. They were too small, too, but her toes felt happier hanging over the edge rather than being crammed inside smelly old canvas.

Even though she was certain the missing crayon wasn't hiding in her room, Frances lifted the bedspreads and looked under both twin beds. Frances searched the desk she shared with her sister, too, all three drawers: hers, her sister's and the one they shared. (Her parents made sure the two girls shared everything equally. Even the bulletin board that hung over the desk was sectioned into halves, Lyndsey had the left and Frances the right.) No missing crayon.

She had to go back to the oak tree. It had to be there.

But she didn't want to go alone.

Frances rode over to MaryEllen Burke's house. MaryEllen seemed a lot older than the rest of the fifth graders. She had a brother who was already in college and her mom had had her when she was pretty old, so it was like Mrs. Burke was making her daughter grow up fast and be old with her. MaryEllen wore horn-rimmed glasses and pointy tennis shoes and parted her hair on the side instead of down the middle. Plus she'd gotten her period in the fourth grade and was allowed to sit out of PE once a month which in a way Frances envied because she hated PE, but no way would she want everyone to know—especially the boys—that she was bleeding there.

MaryEllen wanted to go to the neighborhood playground. "Let's swing," she said.

"Okay, but then I want to go somewhere else," Frances said, but MaryEllen was already on her bike, pedaling toward the playground.

MaryEllen rode her brother's old Schwinn, which was bigger and easily outdistanced Frances's smaller bike. Sweat trickled from MaryEllen's temples, making her brown, side-parted hair look greasy. There was perspiration running down her back, too, and Frances, trailing behind, could see the outline of bra straps through MaryEllen's shirt.

They swung for a while, then MaryEllen wanted to go on the slide, first sitting forward then backward. Bored, Frances suggested they skip the ladder and try climbing up the chute.

"But my hands are kind of sweaty and I might slip."

"Give me your hand, I'll pull you up," Frances offered. MaryEllen was right, her hands were sweaty, but Frances hung on and hoisted the other girl to the top of the slide.

"That was fun!" MaryEllen laughed in Frances's face.

Frances didn't mind the little old lady tennis shoes and the tortoiseshell glasses and even the hairstyle, but MaryEllen's teeth were another story. It didn't look as if she ever brushed them. Rhonda Ottman told Frances once that MaryEllen's mom had fallen down the stairs on her wedding day. The fall had knocked out all her teeth and she had to get dentures. *On her wedding day.* That was why, Rhonda said, Mrs. Burke was such a grumpy old woman now. Since MaryEllen's mom had dentures and didn't have to go to the dentist anymore she never took MaryEllen to the dentist and now her teeth were really gross, like greenish-gray gross, the color you'd get if you blended olive green and cornflower with a little bit of black.

"Let's climb to the top of the monkey bars," Frances said, hoping to get MaryEllen in a more adventurous mood so they could head out to the field and find her crayon.

MaryEllen looked doubtful. "The very top?"

"Sure," Frances said.

"But my hands are still sweaty. I don't want to slip."

"You won't. Once you get to the top, it feels really good 'cause you can feel the breeze."

The metal structure was built as a series of open cubes that telescoped to one square set of bars at the top. Above was nothing but sky. Below was asphalt, black and cracked.

Frances was already more than halfway to the top when MaryEllen finally grabbed hold of the first rung. She put her foot on a rung and the smooth sole of her tennis shoe slipped.

"C'mon," Frances shouted. "You can do it."

MaryEllen reached the second level and her hands slid along the bars, wet and frictionless.

Frances sat on the very top. "I can see your house from here!"

"Really?" MaryEllen had more incentive now and she climbed to the third, the fourth and finally the top level. "Where?"

Frances flipped over and hung from her knees. "I was wrong. It's not your house, just Weird Harold's."

MaryEllen seemed a little mad, probably because Frances had confused her house with Harold Turner's, so to make amends she said, "I really like your hair today."

"Thanks." MaryEllen flicked the damp strands over her shoulders.

Frances swung upright and sat facing her friend in the top cube of the monkey bars. "Let's play this game where we tell each other one thing," she said.

"Like what?" MaryEllen asked.

"Well, you know, one thing that, if you could, you'd change about the other person."

"Anything?"

"Yeah, like—" Frances wanted say she wished they *both* were braver, so they wouldn't be afraid to go out to the big tree in the field, but not on the first round. It would be better to build up to the real thing, so she began with something obvious. "Like, I wish you had a nicer mom."

"Yeah, me too," MaryEllen said and wiped her palms against her Bermuda shorts.

"Now it's your turn."

"Okay, Frank, I wish your nose wasn't so big."

"My nose?" Frances's hand flew to her face.

"Yeah, and I wish you'd stop telling people what to do, like what games to play and what name to call you. You'd probably have more friends if you weren't so bossy. And *everybody* wishes your mother didn't act so stuck up. Is it true she's going to be teaching at our school next year?"

"One thing!" Frances dropped down to the next rung, her face colliding with an iron bar in her haste. She hit her cheekbone so hard it brought tears to her eyes. "You're only supposed to tell one thing." She should have told MaryEllen about her gross teeth. They could just rot out of her head for all she cared. "And don't call me Frank!" she hollered over her shoulder as she jumped on her bike.

Frances pedaled along Davidson Drive with one hand plastered against her face, willing her nose, which she now knew to be too big, to shrink. Stupid MaryEllen. What did she know? Like *she* had so many friends. Frances couldn't help that her nose was too big or that her name was so stupid. She just wanted to go home and draw; color a picture that showed everything the way she'd like it to be. She would draw herself like Joan Walsh Anglund; none of the people in her books had noses; maybe Miss Anglund had a big nose, too. Frances would draw herself standing in front of a giant oak tree, a nose-less creature in a sky blue dress.

But first she had to go to the oak and find the sky blue.

She turned left onto Plantation Drive, the opposite way of home. Bambi King lived on this end of the street. Bambi King, whose real name was Belinda, was super lucky: two great names. Maybe she'd be playing outside when Frances rode by and they could go together to the oak tree because someone as cool as Bambi would not be afraid to walk past the little shacks where people were hiding out from the law and she would totally agree about MaryEllen's teeth being gross and totally disagree about Frances's nose being too big.

But Bambi wasn't out and Frances reached the end of Plantation Drive where it ended in a rumple of asphalt, as if the road crew had emptied their truck there one day and had never returned. Frances propped her bike against the black mound. She climbed over the asphalt onto the dirt track. There was the cluster of shacks barely bigger than her playhouse. She looked for signs of people cooking, eating, doing something. Frances didn't see a single soul, not even a dog. It didn't look as if anyone really lived here at all. Probably no one did and Rhonda Ottman had made it all up. Probably Rhonda Ottman had made up a lot of stuff.

But then a shadow moved at the corner of one of the buildings. "Whatcha doing?"

Frances froze and said, "Nothing."

The shadow moved and Frances could see it was a real flesh and blood person, a man, an oldish kind of man with a scraggly beard, dressed in clothes that had faded to shades of gray and umber. Her knees began to shake, just a little. Rhonda hadn't been lying.

"You don't live round here," he said.

"No." Frances wondered what horrible crime he had committed. Had he not paid his bills? Robbed a bank? Killed someone? Would he kill her? "I'm just passing through," Frances said in a puny voice.

"T'get to where?"

"That big tree," Frances said, pointing off in the distance. "I think I lost one of my crayons there. Over there. Under the tree." Admitting she had come so far to look for such a silly, little thing, she felt her face flush magenta.

"I had some of them once."

"Crayons?"

"Mmm hmm. You got one of them sharpener things in the back?"

Frances nodded.

"They don't work worth spit," he said and then pulled something from his pocket.

It was a knife. Frances felt her knees quake.

"You best be hurrying," the man said as he flicked open the blade.

She tensed, ready to run.

"Looks like rain's blowing in," he said and began picking at his fingernails. "Good luck finding that crayon."

Frances moved fast across the uneven field and it chewed up her feet where they hung over the edge of her too-small sandals. She looked and looked, but there was no sky blue crayon anywhere.

Toes scraped raw, cheek still smarting from where she'd smacked it on the playground, Frances faced the truth: her crayon was lost.

And no one was ever going to call her Francie. With her boring brown eyes, she'd always be stuck wearing ugly brown things. Her awful hair would never hang straight and loose down her back. Bambi King would never be caught dead hanging out with her. Even MaryEllen Burke thought she was a big-nosed, stuck-up, bossy *Frank*.

Frances pedaled home; her head felt like a cartoon bomb, black and ticking. She felt like crying. She was crying, or maybe it was the rain. She dropped her bike against the iron jockey, chipping his apricot face and making a big black scar. Oh great! How was she going to hide that from her mother?

Frances slipped into the bathroom and sprayed Bactine on her feet. The sting of antiseptic helped her not think about MaryEllen Burke and her lost crayon and boils on butts and horrible brown dresses. Her mother found her wrapping Band-Aids around her toes.

"Frances what happened?" her mother asked. "Where have you been?" She held Frances's chin and angled her face toward the light over the sink. "Were you in a fight?"

Frances told the truth, that she'd slipped on the monkey bars and then had hiked to the big tree in the field. But she didn't tell her mother everything, especially not that MaryEllen thought she was stuck up.

"You're not supposed to leave the neighborhood, Frances! The people that live over there are dangerous."

What did she know? Frances doubted she'd ever even been over there.

"Those people, believe me, they'll take everything you have—your bicycle, even your shoes."

I'll give them my shoes, Frances thought, *they're too small anyway. They can take that stupid, scratchy church dress, too.*

"I don't want you going over there again. Understand? Now wash up Frances, you're filthy."

Frances ran the water until it was so hot it steamed the mirror. She liked it foggy, that way she didn't have to look at her huge nose.

When Frances threw her sandals back in the closet they bumped into her old Keds, knocking one over. A sky blue crayon, its point now blunt and rounded, part of its paper sleeve torn, rolled onto the floor.

Frances eased the paper back until it was even and smooth, then twisted sky blue in the hole at the back of the Crayola box. The man was right; the sharpener didn't work well at all. It just chewed the crayon to bits. Frances thought she could do a better job by just coloring and wearing away at the sides. And so she did, making an entire sheet of notebook paper sky blue.

Then she spread all the crayons around her on the floor. She used tan to lightly draw the outline of a girl wearing a long dress that flowed almost to the ground. It had billowy sleeves, and Frances filled them in with white, leaving just a hint of tan showing through so the sleeves looked sheer and grown up. Frances made the top of the dress spring green and the skirt sky blue. She blended a little navy and cadet into the skirt for shadows. Her mother was wrong. Spring green and sky blue were the best combination ever. She took everything off her half of the bulletin board and pinned this new drawing right in the center.

PARANOID, POTENTIALLY bi-polar, Pepsi addict. I would say Coke addict but you would hear white powder, snort-up-your-nose coke with a lower case "c" and I'm talking about capital "C" Coke, the kind with sugar and caffeine. Ridge literally lives on it. That and nicotine. These days he no longer bothers with a cup or a glass, just guzzles the stuff straight from the two-liter bottle and lights another cigarette.

He doesn't eat because he says food makes him sleepy. And the last thing he wants to do is sleep. No, he's got more important things to do, like put the 27th or 33rd, I've lost count, coat of varnish on his dining room floor. You'd think by now he would have hooked up the range that his brother gave him five years ago. But no, on those rare occasions that Ridge actually eats, he just uses his grill. It's in the kitchen.

You're probably thinking: Fire Hazard. But don't worry. He's got running water so he's confident that he could douse the flames in an instant if he had to. Downstairs anyway. He had to turn off the water upstairs, something's wrong with the shower. But he's rigged something in the basement, running the hose from the washing machine over near the drain.

I offered to help him fix the shower last time I was there, but he wasn't having any of that. He wanted to show me the boat he got on eBay or from the impound lot, or maybe it was the twin ATV's he found on Craigslist, I don't remember. He's always got some new toy for the weekends when his son comes to visit. "Anything for the boy," Ridge says. "'Cause you know his mama doesn't do shit for him."

ANYTHING FOR THE BOY

I DON'T KNOW BUT I BELIEVE some people might make their martinis with gin, for instance, Knox's mama Pinky.

Pinky Van Every Devereaux came from old money that had all but evaporated, as much as anything could evaporate in Georgia's humid air. Vestiges of the Van Every fortune clung to her like so much mold. The family home steadily decaying around her, wife of a Baptist deacon, mother of a lesbian and a son who abandoned his daddy's law firm to tangle with Yankees—you don't think this woman had good reason to drink?

Knox Devereaux met Callie Sullivan, born and bred in the City of Broad Shoulders, and promptly fell in love with her Chicago candor, her way of calling a spade a spade. She, in turn, was swept off her feet by his southern charm and how he'd call a spade anything but.

When Knox had invited Callie to Augusta to meet his family, she'd imagined a place perfumed by the soft scent of camellias, a city with grand avenues bordered by live oaks dripping in Spanish moss. Certainly not cramped streets lined by seedy venues with subtitles: DURETTE'S THIS 'N' THAT, A FAMILY AFFAIR and CRAB KING, BEST LEGS IN TOWN—businesses that amazingly shared the same block with the Van Every mansion, a place where Callie held her breath because even the bed sheets smelled of mildew.

"Just call me Mag," Knox's sister Mary Margaret said when introduced to Callie during cocktails on the verandah. "Impressed by our genteel southern manners?" she asked, gesturing toward the far end of the porch where the roof drooped from dry rot, termites or both. "Why, even our house curtseys."

Pinky passed a tray of martinis, and though Callie would

IN THE SOUTH, WE SAY

have preferred a nicely chilled Chardonnay, it was hot and she was thirsty so she took a sip. "Oh my God, Knox!" she gasped. "This tastes like sperm!"

"It's gin," Knox said and flushed scarlet as the pimiento in his olive.

Mag laughed, deep and loud.

Pinky sidled back to Callie, put a gentle hand on her shoulder. "Honey," she whispered, "in the South, we say jizzim."

Aｎｏｔｈｅｒ ｂｅｅ ｄｅａｄ.

Remind, child a joso be better more than hudu, Pasqueline had always said.

And wasn't that the sure truth? Fixing up cures was finer than dabbling in hurt. Better to conjure a charm or two and tend to her neighbor who relied on arrowroot tea and rosemary oil for her swollen joints.

Dead for true. Maggie Bliss moved a box of empty vodka bottles off the chair and sat. She could make out—with her glasses—beads of pollen caught on the delicate fuzz and fur of the bee. Stopped from finishing its job.

Looked like it was napping, that little bee did here on her garden table.

Maggie felt it. Trouble. Hovering in the pines, trembling in the ground. "Oh, for a handful of bird pepper."

Pasqueline would have called for guinea pepper.

Now that the day was noon dusk shade, maybe just a sprinkling along the lot line. Pasqueline would not have hesitated for she'd not been afraid of a little hoodoo when necessary. *Oh, for a handful of guinea pepper,* she'd have said. The most Maggie would do was bird pepper and maybe some sulphur.

It was no use. Everything was dying on the vine. Even she felt withered. Parched. Summer that year had refused to drop away and the line between it and autumn blurred, congealed like old jam. Too much of a good thing, past its prime.

Maggie filled an old washtub with water from the hose. A skinny fox had ventured out of the woods last night to drink from her cat's dish on the porch. "Here you are, Mr. Fox Red," she said and dragged the tub under the oaks.

"Mama! Mama! Where are you?" Bella called across the

GUINEA PEPPER

side yard. "Don't you answer your phone any more?" Maggie's daughter stalked across the lawn and even as she drew closer, didn't lower her voice. "I've been trying to reach you all afternoon. What's that on your face?"

"Tomato." Maggie lifted the tail of her shirt and wiped her face. "I haven't been close enough to hear the phone, I guess."

"Mama, you didn't get it all." Bella grasped her mother's jaw and with her thumb scrubbed the corner of her mouth, flicking a tiny bead of tomato onto the ground. "What have you been doing out here?"

"Picking." Maggie turned away and went back to where she'd left the hose. "What brings you by?" she asked, gathering the hose as she went.

"I have a surprise for you!"

Bella had gained a little weight in the last week; her face seemed softer, but not her voice.

Bella handed her mother a bag, not a gift bag, but a glossy black bag, one with an orange and blue logo on it.

"What is it?"

"A new phone."

"I have a phone."

"Not one like this. This is a cell phone."

"A cell phone? What do I want with one of those?"

"With this, I can reach you whenever, wherever." Bella smoothed her dress over her barely protruding stomach and pouted. "You're going to want to know when it's time for the baby to come, aren't you?"

Bella had waited a long time to have this baby. Nearly forty, she was trying to schedule every step of her pregnancy, just like she time-managed everything else. When the time came, Maggie wouldn't need a phone, but she didn't say that to Bella. "That's months away, child. No need to be worrying about that today."

"But you should learn how to use it now. Let me show you what all it can do." The instruction manual that Bella pulled from the bag was thicker than the phone itself.

Bella tutored Maggie on the basics—on/off, recharging. Even with her glasses, Maggie deemed the numbers too small. It was much easier to use the phone in her kitchen, the one that had been hanging on her wall for years.

"And look Mama, it's so small you can keep it right here. See—" Bella leaned over and dropped it her mother's shirt pocket.

The weight of the phone hung heavy on Maggie's left breast, awkward and uncomfortable, like heartburn, but external.

"Thank you." Maggie itched to remove the phone from her pocket. "Will you stay for supper? Dillie Winchester brought by a raisin pie this morning. I'm fixing to pull some greens and fry some tomatoes."

"Thanks, but no." Bella turned to leave. "Maybe another time." She folded the glossy black bag and smoothed it flat. "What was the pie in payment for?"

"It's scorzonera I'm pulling. You used to like that."

"Mama, what did you do to Dillie Winchester?"

"I didn't *do* anything. She got into some poison ivy at the churchyard and needed a little jewel weed."

"She should've gone to urgent care and gotten a course of prednisone. Some day, Mama, someone's gonna sue you."

"I'm causing no harm, Bella."

"No more voodoo Mama. Do you hear me?"

"*Voodoo?* What do think I'm doing? Sacrificing chickens?"

"What if you do cause some harm, Mama? Some harm that can't be undone." Bella nudged the overgrown grass with the toe of her leather flats. "Have you found anyone to help you around here? Any landscapers? Some painters?"

"I don't need any help. Everything's fine."

"Mama, I mean it. It's past time to paint the house. At least the trim. And the yard is a disaster. You need to make some calls this weekend or I'm sending my lawn service over Monday. Okay?"

After Bella left, Maggie picked up a rake. It wasn't her daughter's threat that prompted her to do so. She enjoyed raking leaves as they fell from these oaks, oaks originally planted to mark a boundary between cotton field and pasture—to provide shade (more for livestock than field hands)—and later as a marker for Ronder Blackwell's smithy.

Back when Ronder achieved his majority, the town of Thorne had yet to be incorporated. Hawthorne College was there of course and had been long before Union blue and Rebel gray had torn each other asunder. By 1879, cotton's fortune again waxed strong and folks scratched their heads wondering why a man like Ronder, muscled and fleet and able to easily pick five bales on his own, chose shoeing horses instead. But Ronder knew two things: one, King Cotton's rule both waxed and waned; and two, while college boys and their professors knew a lot about a lot of things, none of them knew the first thing about blacksmithing. Yet they all owned horseflesh.

Ronder the farrier, who later took the surname Blackwell, grew if not rich, at least comfortable; a surprising feat for a first generation freed black man. He made enough money to build himself a fine two-story frame house on the outskirts of town. When it was time to marry, Ronder Blackwell didn't settle for any local girl but locked his doors for a brace of weeks and rode south to Charleston, to the low country where women were rumored to be more than just passing fair.

As for his bride, none other than Pasqueline McEllis would do. Her family tree was rooted in the islands of the Gullah and grafted with branches of planters, carpetbaggers and horse traders. Pasqueline's brown eyes were ringed with green and she spoke with a low-pitched lyricism seldom heard inland. Ronder the blacksmith was smitten.

Ronder Blackwell's new wife asked her husband to whitewash the house while she painted the doors and the shutters blue, ensuring that no haints, those spirits caught between dead and alive, would dare cross her threshold. Then she planted a garden that seemed to flourish overnight;

strange scents wafted from the smoke in her fires. Sunday morning conversations at Hawthorne Presbyterian, whispered behind funeral parlor fans, held that Pasqueline McEllis Blackwell conjured her own climate, one conducive to growing mysterious things unheard of in the Carolina backcountry. That didn't stop women from calling on her, seeking cures for what ailed them.

— • —

Bella returned Tuesday with a bag of groceries. "Mama, I've got some coconut oil for you. It's supposed to be good for your memory. I'm guessing you already lost the phone I got you, didn't you?"

Maggie hadn't lost it. She just didn't want to use it. She didn't particularly want to use coconut oil either.

"I brought you some kale and some organic chicken so you can have a healthy dinner tonight. Also—" Bella opened the refrigerator and put her hand on her hip. "Mama, don't tell me you have fat back in here."

"Okay, I won't," Maggie said. "And don't you tell me how to keep my kitchen."

"Don't think I didn't see all those vodka bottles the other day."

"I'm distilling lavender."

"For heaven's sake, who does that, Mama?"

"I do," Maggie said. "Storm's brewing."

"Mama, you're crazy. How can you possibly think a storm's coming when we are in the middle of the worst drought we've had in nearly a century?" Bella stowed the kale and the chicken and a carton of brown eggs in her mother's refrigerator. Then, mission accomplished, she prepared to leave. "Remember, Friday we're going to visit Mrs. Meachum. She's invited us for lunch."

Maggie had forgotten.

"I'll pick you up around a quarter to ten!"

Maggie followed her daughter to her car, hoping to think of a reason to change their plans. Before she could, Bella left with a cheery little wave.

The Grove. Maggie had no desire to visit anyone at that place, least of all Gloria Meachum. She knew why Bella had arranged this visit. As if Maggie would ever consider moving.

To her way of thinking, Gloria had just given up. Given up and let her son take over. "Just think, with a condo," Bella had said, "you'd have absolutely no worries." No worries for whom? Maggie wanted to know. Of course Gloria's son wasn't worrying now—he'd transferred that right to the staff at The Grove. It was now their duty to see that his mother was fed and occupied, their obligation to see that her room was clean, that her bowels were regular. She doubted that Gloria was worry-free. Wouldn't she be worrying about whether she still had any purpose in this life? Any reason to get up out of that worry-free bed at The Grove?

One lone crow swooped overhead. Shrieking, choking on words charred black as his feathers. Six more followed, silent in its wake. Maggie pulled more scorzonera, digging into the dry clay where the roots threaded deep into the earth. Few appreciated this vegetable any more. But look how handsome its long purple roots looked against the mulch, mulch that had once been dark and loamy, now dried to silvery grey.

Maggie plucked a tomato, crushed it against her mouth and smeared the pulp of it across her chin, down her neck and across her chest, tiny yellow seeds stuck in the crevasses of her skin, those paths of time. She pulled stinging nettle, boneset and verbena and crushed their leaves be-tween her palms, held them to her nose as if she could ever forget the spicy dark smell of them. She called them by their Latin names, because she could, an old woman whom others dared assume was past her prime. She knew their Latin particulars and their potencies. She knew which seeds were curative and which roots nourished and which ones were pure poison. Should she choose, she could consign anyone on this street to his fate, with no more thought than deadheading a bed of chrysanthemums.

— • —

In 1916, when trouble came, Ronder and his wife were ready. Together they drove their horse and mule into higher pastures, moved the chickens, picked vegetables early. They took their tables, their chairs, the bed ticking, the footboard, the headboard, carried it all upstairs and stowed it in the attic. They were ready when the river rose forty feet and more over its banks, taking farms, houses, a cotton mill.

As a child, Maggie had never tired of listening to Pasqueline's stories, and the story of the flood, almost Biblical in its proportions, was her favorite of all. She hadn't *seen* the flood coming, Pasqueline explained to her granddaughter.

Using the ball, Maggie learned, was more a matter of simple arithmetic, putting two and two together. "Child, I look here and only here," and Pasqueline would point one long and bony finger at the center of the ball, "and I be thinking on all the things in the everyday that I see and I hear. When I sit quiet, the important signs, they come together."

"How did you know what the important things were before the flood came?" Maggie asked.

Pasqueline told her granddaughter that she listened to both man and nature. When Ronder said he'd heard at the barbershop that hooded men were riding at night and burning crosses, she listened. Ladies from the church asked was Ronder heading to Chicago with the others? The birds and the squirrels, too, had things to tell her. "They be going tree high and never did they come down," Pasqueline said. "And, chicken thief, Mr. Fox Red, he that be always sniffin' for my chickens by the light of the moon, he be gone." She said that the sunflowers and honeysuckle remained untouched; no deer came anywhere near.

"Why Ma'lina?" Maggie asked, "Where were the fox and the deer?"

"Vanished."

Maggie loved this part of the story, loved how her grandmother said that word, three syllables, van-ish-ed. As if from another world, another time. "What did you do then ma'lina? Did you make Grandpa Ronder hunt the deer and bring them back?"

"No child. The sky, I leaned my ear against. The sky it were so still, like a body, a kuwfa, with no more breath left in its bones."

"And then what?"

"I be more quiet. More than the sky quiet. Only then I hear the wind coming two directions at one and the same time. From the south and from the east."

"In the winter when that happens it means snow, right?"

Pasqueline nodded and stroked Maggie's plaits. "Clouds they be coming light and fast, sun high."

"How did you know what was going to happen?"

"Me, I not can say. But when no honest man crack his teeth and only d' man with d' big eye say everything be fine—goma weather come. Bad things, they happen then."

"Why didn't you stop the flood, Ma'lina?"

"Oh child, water be God's way of takin' away the clap-trap and devils from this world and there be times we be called on to help."

Maggie wanted to know what to look for and what to listen for— when the time came for her to help.

Begin quiet was always Pasqueline's advice. *Be still.*

Maggie had trouble with that, even at this advanced stage of impending grandmotherhood. She felt the ball calling to her, trying to claim her attention. But she ignored it. Though she had coveted her grandmother's crystal sphere as a child, Maggie feared it as an adult.

Pasqueline had never used it with outsiders; she never claimed to be clairvoyant and did not want to be called a fortuneteller. She'd let Maggie handle it a bit, letting her granddaughter pretend to see the new doll or the pony cart she wished for in its depths. But when Maggie once rolled it about on the kitchen floor, like a giant marble, Pasqueline lost her temper. "Child, what you do? This thing, it not be for playing of that kind!"

Maggie, frightened by the tone in her grandmother's voice, snatched the ball off the floor and stood quickly. Too quickly. She lost her balance and the ball slipped from her hand, landed hard on the floor and rolled under the icebox.

Neither Maggie's nor Pasqueline's arms were long enough to reach it. They had to wait until Ronder came in for dinner.

When he pulled the ball from its dusty hiding place, they discovered that it had cracked at its core. The crack splintered into a half-dozen spidery veins but did not reach the surface.

"Ma'lina, I'm so sorry. I'm so sorry," Maggie repeated over and over long past the sun's setting.

"*Bahn*. The worst, it is done."

But the worst, it seemed, was to follow. The well went dry and digging a new one sorely strained Ronder's heart. The attack didn't kill him, but it took the life out of him all the same.

Maggie washed the ball in watered down brandy as she had seen her grandmother do. She tried every conjure and kafu she'd ever heard to repair it. But there was no going back to the way things had been.

Every afternoon for weeks after she'd sit gazing at the ball, losing herself while looking at the distortions refracted and reflected through the damaged glass.

One day while she studied the darkest vein of the imperfection, she imagined a storm, clouds the color of a bruise on her knee. Lightning took shape, jagged, mirroring the cracks in the sphere itself.

Hours later, Pasqueline found her on the back porch steps, the ball in her lap, hands at her temples, her back bowed in the shape of a "C." "Child, shake your feet before this storm it strike you dead!"

The urgency in Pasqueline's voice frightened Maggie from her trance. The sky was the color of eggplants, divided by silver streaks of lightning. Stinging needles of rain, fast and furious, bit into her arms. Maggie was never certain if she'd conjured that storm or had foreseen it.

— • —

Here it was late October, and *slap*, there were still flies out and about. It was late for them to be so hard at work. For that matter it was getting too late in the season for *her* to be so hard at work. The fact she was out here in the yard working so hard should make Bella happy. Lord knows the visit to The Grove hadn't made anyone happy—a disaster from start to finish. Maggie twisted the pitchfork, lifting and turning half-rotted leaves, stirring lime into the compost.

She had spent the early morning forking the richest mulch from the bottom of the bin and had moved several wheelbarrows' worth to the side yard. She heard a truck pull up and knew it was the Caldwell brothers. There was no rush; they knew exactly where she wanted the sand. In a few minutes she'd meet them with this last bit of mulch and together they'd mix sand and compost into the bed where her poppies grew.

Except there was no Caldwell Quarry dump truck parked in her side yard. Instead, there was a white panel van in her drive, ladders tied to its roof. Maggie took the pitchfork and went around the house to investigate.

Two men in painters' whites were on her porch, her porch now draped in white canvas dropcloths. An open can of black paint sat between them. One was scraping blue paint from her shutters, the other was already painting.

"What are you doing?" she asked.

The man holding the paintbrush turned toward her and said, "Ma'am?"

She raised her voice and pointed the handle of the pitchfork at him, "What are you doing?"

"You Miz Bliss, right?"

"I am, but I never did ask anyone to paint my shutters black."

"Oh this ain't black, ma'am. Lots of folks make that mistake. This here is Charleston Green. It's pretty, too, when the sun hits it just right."

"I don't want my trim green, black, or purple. It's blue, always has been, always will be."

"Your girl said that this was gonna be a surprise—"

"I don't care what my daughter told you. You're going to make that shutter the color it was before you walked your sorry selves onto my front porch and then you're gonna get gone."

"But ma'am, she's done paid us to paint everything Charleston Green. You wait and see. Everything'll be just fine once we're done."

"Paint it blue." Maggie speared the lawn with the tines of her pitchfork. "Paint it blue. And then get out of here."

"Now look here ma'am, your girl said to get it done before the week was over because there's a Realtor coming to appraise your property Saturday. Plus, it ain't like we got blue paint with us today. It'll be on into next week before we'll be painting anything blue."

"Then, pack up and get out of here. Now."

"But don't you want it to look nice for the Realtor?"

"If you aren't packed up and off my porch in two minutes, I'll have you arrested for trespassing."

The other man had already stopped scraping and was folding dropcloths as fast as he could. Chips of faded gullah blue fell into the vinca that bordered the porch. In his haste, he pulled the last cloth before his partner had secured the lid on the paint can.

Maggie watched the oily black river spread across the porch floor. She climbed the porch steps, swinging the pitchfork at the two painters who were unable now to move, to do anything but watch the disaster spreading before them. "Get out!" The paint dripped down one step, and then another. "Get out." As sunlight hit the paint, it did look green, like poison.

Maggie smoothed a fresh cloth over the table near the kitchen window.

In a nest of linen towels in the pantry, between mason jars filled with dried herbs, snakeskins and crushed alum, pyrite and quartz, curled a white cat. Her ears lay flat against her head, and her tail, ermine-tipped, twitched, tapping against a glass ball. Though it was warm to the touch, a chill slipped along the length of Maggie's spine as she transferred it to the table.

Hah! the ball seemed to say and rolled away from her, seeking a groove worn into the center of the table. A ray of light hit its center, blinding Maggie for a moment.

She rolled the ball back and through the glass the cloth's threads appeared distorted, crooked and uneven.

At first, the ball showed only the inverted reflection of the kitchen window, the sill at the top of the ball. Each of the window's rectangular panes fanned out, wider at the base. The sphere caught blue sky and trees; tree limbs became one with the cracks that emanated from the center of the ball. The cat sprang onto the table. One paw tapped the ball. It rolled away, and the image of the window disappeared. Maggie put the cat on the floor.

Focus. She could hear Pasqueline's voice.

Now the ball's center glowed pink and amber, the color of rose gold. The tree limbs again took shape within the cracked glass.

The curve of a woman's shoulder formed among the trees while a black mass seemed to bloom at the top of the sphere. From the center, light burst, dazzled. Sparks seemed to explode from every crack within.

Again the curve of shoulder, and then a wing. A gnat, a fly, a wasp. Maggie's own reflection stared at her from inside the glass. Never before had she seen herself within the sphere.

Her place was here. All this—the ball, the table, the house and the knowledge coursing through her veins would pass to her granddaughter —Bella's daughter. It must.

Maggie took a knot of angelica root from one of the pantry drawers, a snakeskin and a bit of kuwfa dust—graveyard dirt. She needed a little ash, powdered sulfur, salt, and yes, guinea pepper. Pasqueline's voice whispered in her ear, *Knuckle be best.* Clap-hats, gafus, the devils of the world, their secrets were revealed in their joints. Maggie opened an old wooden cask, and breathed in its musty scent. She tested one bone, then another, massaging their every knob. With a length of twine she bound bone and root together, covered them with the fine yellowish-grey dust. *Fasten the jar most tightly. Wrap it in a piece of old black cloth, heavy, make it wool or felt and bury it at middle night.*

It took some time to bury the jar. The ground was hard and dry and the shovel met with great resistance, but it was no match for Maggie's resolve. A scant wisp of a cloud drifted and parted over a slivered moon and the night was quiet, the sky pitch.

The next morning, the wind came in waves, at first hushed, then building in volume and intensity until it swirled in great gusts. Twigs, some with small clusters of leaves still attached, spiraled to the ground.

The scent of minerals filled the air, evidence that moisture was being pulled from the soil. Iron, mica, sulphur, rose from the ground and mixed with the clouds overhead. Thunder moaned, but the winds died back, exhausted. They rested, gathered strength, and tried again to muster a storm. After an hour of repeated attempts, the heavens gave up.

Every door, every window, Maggie opened, letting out anything that wanted, needed, to escape. Along the wood's edge she checked for signs of the thirsty red fox. He was gone. No sign of the crows, either.

She leaned her ear against the sky. It stood still. She heard, ever so faintly, the wind coming two directions at one and the same time. From the south and from the east. Clouds were coming—light and fast, sun high. Three geese flew north, fast and low to the ground.

Maggie lifted her face to the sky and tasted a metallic dampness in the air. A scent of sulphur. Lightning in the west. Clouds converged. The sky grew darker, the color of slate. The air grew chill. Maggie stood still, willing every droplet of moisture loose from the sky. She stood there until she was soaked to the bone.

E VADENE AND Weldon Tuttle loved that old chair. It was the first and one of the onliest things they'd ever bought new. Eight dollars it had cost and they paid for it over time. A quarter a week. Thirty-two weeks, more than half a year. Long about June, Bob Cashion just let them take it on home. He knew they were good for the last buck. And you know, Evadene nor Weldon neither one sat in that chair for four weeks until they owned it free and clear. Truth was, it was enough just to look at it, sitting in the front room, the parlor Evadene took to calling it once the chair was installed there near the window. Rose-colored brocade with mauve gimp. Carved mahogany arms and legs. And in July when that chair was done paid for, they took turns sitting in it. "Weldon, I do believe it's your turn this evening," Evadene would say on a Monday. Then on Tuesday, "Have a seat, my dear," Weldon would say to his bride.

So to see the chair outside, waiting for the Salvation Army men to come and collect it, near about broke Sylvia's heart. It wasn't right for something so dearly loved to be left like trash on the porch.

About a week later, after visiting Evadene at the nursing home, Sylvia stopped at the Salvation Army. There was the chair sitting with a lumpy blue sofa and a floor lamp made out of an old wagon wheel. Sylvia checked for a price tag. A piece of masking tape with $8 written in blue marker covered a worn spot in the upholstery.

Sylvia figured it was a sign and she paid the volunteer clerk who had brassy beehive hair and half glasses that dangled on a chain around her neck. Sylvia counted out a five and three ones, somehow wedged that chair in the trunk of her car

STRAYS

and drove home at about five MPH, hazard lights flashing.

Just wasn't right for something once so cherished to be abandoned Sylvia thought as she waited for the microwave to finish cooking her Lean Cuisine.

She tried the chair first in one corner, then the other. Found she liked it best near the window, facing out. She could sit there and watch the birds and the squirrels and the kids across the street.

"I believe it's your turn this evening, Thomasina," she said to the calico cat who had appeared on her porch last March. The cat also liked to sit by the window and watch the birds and the squirrels and the kids across the street.

The children were about four and five or thereabouts. Their mama, Sylvia heard, had up and walked out on them. *How could a woman do that?* Sylvia wondered. Just wasn't right to abandon those children and that fine man. Well, Sylvia assumed he was a fine man. He always took time to make sure the children were buckled in the backseat of that beat up old Volvo wagon whenever they went out. And they went out most evenings round about dinner time. Sylvia would sit in her chair and eat her Lean Cuisine or a Hot Pocket and about an hour later, they'd pull back in the drive and that fine man would lean into the back seat and unbuckle those children. Some nights he'd have to carry the littler one in and Sylvia would watch her curly head nod and bob on his shoulder.

Wasn't right. Wasn't right and that's when Sylvia got the notion to invite them to dinner.

MOMSTER
Hang in there -- take one day at a time.
wrap your brain around what you
have to do to make it to lights out.
love you.10/28 10:53 AM

#1 SON
Wise words mother but there is no lights out.
cpt spears turns em on whenever he wants
to.1. 3. 4. then for real at 5. jack 10/28 6:22 PM

MOMSTER
At least you get a half hour of
phone time. and you didn't get
kicked out.10/28 6:25 AM

#1 SON
I just found out they are not letting me out
for thanksgiving my favorite holiday. the
one that i would drive to your house when
i am thirty to celebrate with you. miss you
jack 10/29 6:13 PM

MOMSTER
Beautiful image -- you driving here on
the 4th thurs of nov when you are 30. if it is
not in the cards then future Thanksgivings
will be all the more precious. xoxo.
10/29 6:15 PM

#1 SON
Had to swim a couple miles today with
weights. on arms and legs. 10/29 6:20 PM

MOMSTER
You will be very fit when you finish
with this. xo 10/29 6:24 PM

#1 SON
Had to stand all day with full pack including
rifle. 10/30 6:14 PM

CON•TEXT

MOMSTER
Even in class? are you tired? do you have
to stand to do homework too?
10/30 6:16 PM

#1 SON
No treats for me today. got to move rocks from
one field to another. Then back. in the rain.
one crappy halloween.10/31 6:14 PM

MOMSTER
I'll save you some reeses. your sister says hi
from oz. she is dressed up as dorothy. how
many more days of this do you have? xo
10/31 6:14 PM

#1 SON (+4344322481)
2 tired 2 tell u what i did today. involved
stairs. and a whistle and some dogs. idk how
many more days. spears won't tell me. tell
pookie hi from me. jack 11/1 6:27 PM

MOMSTER
You can do it. Hang in there.
Love you.11/1 6:29 PM

#1 SON
Good news!!! cpt. spears said that if i get through
whatever they make me do tomorrow i can
get a pass for the weekend. so i was hoping
that i could hitch a ride to Roanoke with one of
the post bacs. if it is alright with you i feel
like i need to get away from the military
scene for a day or two. so pretty please?
i love you jack 11/2 6:01 PM

MOMSTER
Jack - i don't think this is a good idea.
which post bac? the one who brought
in the vodka?11/2 6:03 PM

#1 SON
No. that dude is history. this guy just
had the nyquil. he's cool. so can I go? i
will love you till the stars turn cold.
11/2 6:09 PM

MOMSTER
I would hope you'll love me till the
stars turn cold regardless of my granting
permission to go to Roanoke or not. xo
11/2, 6:12 PM

MOMSTER
maybe i'll come up and take
you out to eat over the weekend
-- how about that?
11/2, 6:15 PM

#1 SON
I don't know....i dont think that i have any free
time. but if you do come up you have
got to take me to dicks in danville!
b-ball season starts soon and my
shoes are worn out. or i can do some
research online and find a shoe
that i like and you can order them for me
and have them sent up here. please email
spears so i can have the wkend pass ok?
11/2 6:29 PM

#1 SON
well you don't have to worry about anything
because spears was playing mind games. i
still have 2 weeks of moto and then
i will have to do a lot of tours and
i can only do them on weekends and free time.
but i can come home for thanksgiving because
they are closing the academy and nobody can stay.
so i will see you then.
11/3, 6:00 PM

"TWO DOLLARS, Lute Jackson," she hollered, "and not a drop more!" Mother Franklin, sixty-six years old and measuring about that many inches around, stepped out of the car. She seemed an improbable mother. But the breadth of her stance, the strength of her gaze, and her righteous discovery of a handkerchief from within her square black pocketbook lent partial credence to the title which was given to her years ago when she might have had children, but had chosen not to. Instead she mothered flocks of children, God's children.

She drew attention standing there in her sateen purple dress that looked more like a choir robe than regular street clothes. Even pleated like it was, the dress strained at every seam. Everything about her was big—her feet, her neck, even her elbows. Her very breath was big and heavy. She stood there as if she needed a tugboat to get moving.

Mother Franklin fanned her face and kept an eye on the gas pump while Luther walked around to the front of the saggy gray station wagon and raised the hood. Luther was as skinny as she was fat. They looked like a black Jack Spratt and his wife, except no one would think they were married—mother and son, maybe. He was at once dutiful and threatening. Seeing them together on the street, people might wonder, would he be nice and offer his arm, or push her from behind?

"This ol' heap'd do better if we just filled the tank all the way every once and again," he said.

"You ain't no trained mechanic, Luther."

"There's gone be some serious trouble here soon enough," he said and slammed the hood shut. "How you be able to keep a driver if your car ain't even runnin'?"

"You just pokin' around under there trying to put the fear

in me." Mother Franklin was tired of his dire predictions, all his complaining. He'd been pestering her for a little cash in his pocket, too, but she was smarter than that. Even here at this filling station she kept the money in her pocketbook, not handing it over until he was done pumping. "Brother Pomeroy, he be a good man. He fix us up once we get to Charlotte."

"Charlotte? That's another week. I ain't waiting that long."

She was tired of his threatening to quit, too. He ought to be more grateful. He was lucky she'd hired him as her driver. Without her, he'd be starving on the side of the road. All she had to do was say, *My driver. A plate for my driver*, and didn't the church ladies provide? That wasn't begging, no matter what Luther said. She didn't beg; she just knew how to ask.

She pulled two one-dollar bills from her purse. "Go on and pay now," she said knowing Luther was in a hurry to be on his way. Lute Jackson liked staying on the move. He liked not knowing where he'd be from week to week because if he didn't know, then no one else did either.

"What church we doin' tonight?" Luther asked when they were back on the road.

"Prophesy Lutheran," Mother Franklin said.

"Maybe you can get them to give us another car."

"They have them some money. Got plumbing and a real nice organ."

"Who cares about plumbing?" Luther said. "You too fat to squeeze into the stalls anyways."

"You hush your sorry mouth, Lute Jackson."

"Them thighs of yours, they got so much meat you needin' someone to reach between there and hold the flesh away from your stream."

Mother Franklin folded her hands across her purse and said nothing.

"I'm tellin' you, I'm done slopping piss. Just 'cause you so fat don't mean I have to be no damned orderly."

"You be whatever I say," Mother Franklin said.

"I say no man should be attendin' to that," Luther said. "You gotta get yourself some girl to help you."

"That wouldn't be nothin' but trouble." Mother Franklin looked at him hard.

"I be your driver, that's all."

"I speak with Brother Pomeroy when we get to Charlotte."

"Charlotte? You always talkin' like Charlotte's gone fix everything. Ain't gone make you no skinnier."

"The good Lord, he done make me this way," Mother Franklin said. "And the good Lord done made you to be my right hand, Lute Jackson."

"Do not quote Ezekiel at me, woman!"

"O unhallowed wicked one, exalt that which is low and abase that which is high."

"Jesus, Lord, deliver me!" Luther said, pounding the steering wheel.

"A ruin, ruin, ruin, I will make of thee," Mother Franklin sang out. A little further down the road she said, "No Jesus up in heaven gone rescue you, Luther."

— • —

Tyrell was fussing and the baby was hungry. Her milk was gone. *What am I gone feed that Jo-Jo now?* "Make up some of that cereal with water, Willie June," Gussie said. "Spoon it up for him."

"But he spit that right out, Mama," Willie June said.

"Don't matter. Just slide it back in again." Gussie licked her finger then touched it to the iron to see if it was hot enough. "How'd all them black marks get on the back of your shirt, Gaynelle?"

"She be sitting in the dirt, listenin' to more of Gwen's stories," Willie June tattled on her little sister.

Gaynelle said, "Ain't nothin' wrong with listenin' to Gwen. She be tellin' me about her boyfriend."

Every day when Gwen got home from work the neighbor girls treated her like the Queen of Sheba—Gwen sitting on an old stuffed chair on the front stoop and the little girls sitting at her feet, painting her toenails, fanning her face.

Every day Gussie had to listen to Gaynelle going on about how Gwen was just the finest lady, her skin like cocoa, shiny and fine; her hair sleek as a seal's. Gaynelle wanted to be just like her. "Whyn't you make my hair straight, Mama, like Gwen's 'stead of all these short, sticky-up pigtails?"

Seemed as if Gaynelle would do anything for Gwen. And as their neighbor's belly grew, "Fetch me another cup full of that fine red dirt, Gaynelle," she'd say and Gaynelle would run over to the hill where she knew the dirt was good, not too wet, not too dry, but just right, like Goldilocks and those three bears. Gaynelle said that she was the only one who knew how to fetch Gwen dirt, like she was the most special servant to the queen.

Today Gaynelle said, "Mama, I want some boy to tell me I'm a ripe little peach and he gone eat me up for dinner."

"Why you wanna be ate up, Gaynelle?" her sister asked. "Gurgling around in some boy's stomach? That's stupid."

"I ain't stupid, Willie June! Got me a one hundred on my handwriting paper last week of school. That ain't stupid."

"Hush," Gussie said and sprinkled starch on another shirt. "You ain't stupid, Gaynelle. But don't you be dreaming 'bout no boys. You too young for that foolishness."

The girls, both thinking they'd won the argument, stuck out their tongues at each other as soon as their mama turned away.

Gussie really didn't care too much what Gaynelle dreamed about, she just wished that girl would sleep. She told Brother Pomeroy just this afternoon, "Lord, but that child be scared of the dark. In the night she be scared and in the daylight she be hungry."

"Don't they feed her lunch at school?" Brother Pomeroy asked.

"Yessir, and if I could get her there on time why they give that hungry mouth breakfast, too. But not now, not in the summertime when no school's in session."

"I hear now they talking 'bout postponing school this fall."

"Lord, I don't need that."

"All that messing in the schools," Brother Pomeroy said. "Moving them childrens here and them childrens there, all so they can make a pretty picture mixing black with white. No sir, no school 'til they have all the 'signments made. You got your girls' 'signments yet, Gussie?"

"No, Lord and why be worrying about it? They been messing with this since I can remember."

"You right about that. Lord, almost twenty years. Since the fifties, when they picked little Dorothy to go to Harding."

"And didn't they just spit on her 'til she gave up and moved away?" But Gussie knew that school would start soon enough. "The girls'll be needing paper and paste and dresses. And shoes pro'ly, too."

"Who gone sit with the boys while you sit with that old man at your work?"

"Willie June is good. A good girl. Does whatever her mama asks. Gaynelle, now she nothing but a handful of nonsense. She can run on to school, but Willie June, Willie June can mind the boys."

"You thinkin' every day?"

"No. Just some. How else I gone put food on the table? And keep the lights on?"

"Gussie, why you stay down here in Charlotte? Go on up and stay with your sister and her family."

Gussie was having none of that. "Stay with my sister and her childrens and my mama, too? I'll just turn off more lights. Watch my pennies. The old man he say he'd give me a bonus. Say no one do for him like Gussie. I'll get me a little bonus—put it to the side."

And Lord, Gussie thought, *when that bonus come in, I'm gone take my-*

self down to the Top Inn, buy me a chicken box, and I ain't sharin' it with no one. Just find me a patch of sun and suck the meat right off the bones. Suck them bones dry…

— • —

Gussie could hear the neighbor girl Perina Turner sassing with Gaynelle in the side yard while they waited for Gwen to get home.

"Hey Gaynelle, who was 'at man over there on your mama's porch this afternoon?" Perina asked. "That your daddy?"

"Perina Turner, why you make me so mad? Every man you see on the street, *Ooh, Gaynelle, that your daddy?* You think you so smart, with your big fat daddy, but you ain't."

"Least I got me a daddy what brings us food. Otherwise, I'd be all scrawny like you."

"Some day I'm gone be big and fine like Gwen. And I'll stay in a fine house with my fine baby's daddy. And we won't name our baby girl after no dog food neither. 'Sides it was the preacher man, Brother Pomeroy come by today."

"Ooh, he done come to save your mama's soul," Perina squealed.

"So what?" Gaynelle said. "Don't yours need savin'?"

In a way Brother Pomeroy had come offering salvation. He'd come offering Gussie Munroe a deal. One that was going to put some food on her table.

"C'mon in here, Gaynelle. Time for supper."

"This lady only gone be here a short while," Gussie explained to her girls later that evening as they moved a stack of clothes from the girls' front room into the one their mama and the boys shared.

The math didn't add up for Willie June. "Five peoples in one room don't seem fair, Mama," she said.

"Won't be five. You girls'll have this bed. I be sleeping out on the sofa."

"You can stay in your bed, Mama. I'll sleep out on the sofa," Willie June said.

Gaynelle said, "You just wanna be watching t.v. all night."

"Girls, you 'member Mother Franklin," Gussie said. "She and her boy Luther, they come round here every couple of years or so for praying camp. She be doing the Lord's work and when we help her, we doing the Lord's work, too."

Gaynelle and Willie June looked at each other. Gaynelle did not remember Mother Franklin. Willie June did.

"Why she stayin' *here* Mama?" Willie June asked. "We ain't hardly got enough for the five of us."

"'Cause Brother Pomeroy, he asked us to make a place for her."

"What'll we feed *her*?"

"Other ladies be bringing by the food and all of us is to share. Good food. Sweet potatoes, turnip greens, chicken."

"And cake?" Gaynelle asked.

"Maybe," Gussie said.

"Yeah," Willie June said, "but that Mother Franklin, she pro'ly be the onliest one to eat any of it."

Gussie shooed the girls outside, "Go on and play."

"Can I go over to Prissy's?" Willie June asked.

"Prissy and Perina? Why you wanna go there?" Gaynelle said, "They so nasty they eat snails right out their yard."

Gussie frowned at her daughter. "Stop telling stories, child."

"It ain't no story if it's the truth."

Gussie knew it was true, she'd seen Mr. Turner out there in his yard looking for snails even though their yard was mostly filled with cars instead of grass. He was always parking some fine old Cadillac or Lincoln over there. Their house was so full of things it spilled onto their porch and filled the carport.

Even though his two girls always had rags tied over their heads, weren't they always pointing out the fine cars their daddy drove and how they had all this stuff—more than Gaynelle and her sister Willie June had for sure.

Once Gaynelle asked her mother why they didn't have more things and Gussie said, "I'd rather have me one or two fine things 'stead of tons of junk."

"But I ain't got nothing. Perina say I ain't even got no daddy."

"You tell that girl everybody got a daddy," she told her daughter. "They just all can't be living with they children."

— • —

An old gray station wagon, riding low to the pavement, stopped in front of Gwen's place. Mother Franklin waited until Luther came around and pulled her out. She stood near the curb, catching her breath, and watched two young girls pay court around an armchair that was losing its stuffing. A pretty young woman sat in the chair, accepting their attention like royalty. Arms gestured, giggles erupted. A little boy, about three years old, hid behind the chair, pulling at the springs that had eaten through the underside. The slap and thud of a fly swatter on the flabby upholstery seemed to muffle their voices against the heavy August air, milky blue above the row of small brick houses.

Mother Franklin said, "Now, look there Lute."

Luther wasn't interested. "They too young."

"Some girls, they grow up fast."

There were two more girls across the street. They were a little older, maybe nine; one had a baby slung around her middle, the other, frisking her hips, made a plastic hoop defy gravity. She caught sight of Mother Franklin and the awful solemn gravity of the old woman pulled that hoop down around the girl's ankles. It seemed as if the hoop moved in slow motion—over the girl's narrow, untried hips, past her knees, finally coming to rest on her bare feet.

Mother Franklin wiped her handkerchief across her broad forehead, suddenly seeming darker and broader, like a ship setting sail against the afternoon sky. She took a few short steps forward, waving the square white cloth with deliberate calm in front of her face, one widespread hand holding her black purse and the other near her face, hiding it from view as if to say coyly and impossibly, *Don't pay no attention to me.*

"Hey!" she tried to get their attention, but her voice came out first in a wheezy whisper. "I be looking for Gussie Munroe's place. Y'all know it?"

The little girls jumped off the porch, leaving the pretty woman in the chair unattended. Surprised someone as old and ugly as Mother Franklin could command such attention, the young woman pushed herself up and out of her chair and disappeared into the house. The little boy, startled by the slam of the screen door, skittered down from the porch and followed his sister and her friend. The two older girls crossed the street.

Mother Franklin looked at the girl holding the baby and said, "I 'member you. Willie June, right?"

"Yes, ma'am."

One of the younger girls pushed up against baby. "I'm Gaynelle and this here's Tyrell."

"You all Gussie's children, then. She here?"

"No, ma'am." Willie June wanted to do the right thing, but she was unsure of what that might be. "She still at work."

"Me and Lute, we need to get settled." Mother Franklin stuffed her handkerchief back inside her purse.

"He staying with us, too?" Gaynelle asked.

"No, child. But he need to carry my things to your mama's before he settles his own self."

Luther held a suitcase in one hand and a paper sack in the other. "That your place?" he asked nodding toward the house next to Gwen's.

"Yes, but no one's home," Willie June said.

"You home, ain't you?"

There wasn't but a little bitty side yard between one house and another, wide enough only for a couple of clotheslines, but it took many long minutes to walk the distance. Panting, Mother Franklin seemed to take several breaths per footfall. One; and then another.

Even though their mama had said not to let anyone in the house when she was at work, Willie June and Gaynelle let Lute carry Mother Franklin's belongings into their room.

The house, never big, shrank to what felt like old clothes, the ones that didn't fit any more and were left at the collection boxes in the church basement.

Her suitcase unpacked, Mother Franklin sat in the front room and the act of sitting took a great deal of time. She didn't sit so much as she leaned into the sofa. She tried to rest her pocketbook on her lap but it slid over the folds of purple sateen covered fat and landed on the floor.

She said, "Lute, you best get yourself over to church now. Be sure to fetch a pillow for the place where I'll be setting. Can't stand no hard seats no more."

"Yes, ma'am."

Gaynelle said, "Why she call you Loot? You got bags of money or something in that old car?"

"M'name ain't *Loot*. It's Luther, but some they call me Lute on account of my singing."

"Why?"

"Cause when he sings, child, it's like hearing the lute of an angel," Mother said.

"Whyn't you sing something right now?" Gaynelle said.

"You too bossy girl." Her head came up to his belt. He could have laid his palm flat on her head and felt her spongy hair all caught up in plastic baubles.

— • —

Usually, when she had company, Gussie put a cloth on her kitchen table. The table, topped with aqua linoleum, was scarred by years' worth of dull knives, sweaty glasses and forgotten cigarettes. But tonight she'd scorched a hole right through that tablecloth. The iron was over hot. The children were fussing, at each other, at her, at nothing save the heat and their empty bellies. Miz Roberts was late getting there with dinner.

Gussie wondered where she'd find another tablecloth as fine as the one she'd ruined. *Why you bother, Gussie?* her sister had asked her a while back. *No one be wasting time ironing no more.* But for Gussie, there was comfort in freshly washed shirts and clean towels and pants with sharp creases. She brought in a little extra money doing laundry for other folks. They liked everything pressed and crisp. This evening, just outside the back door, in the strip of yard between her place and Gwen's, men's shirts and pants hung on a length of white cotton cord gone grey, waiting for a hot iron and starch.

The old table, much too large for the small kitchen, sat in front of a noisy Frigidaire. An electric stove with two working burners was wedged between the sink and a narrow run of counter top. Above this hung a row of cabinets, doors long gone. Tonight Jo-Jo's high chair and chairs for her and Tyrell and the girls faced each other across the long sides of the scarred table. Mother Franklin would sit at the head.

Miz Roberts finally arrived with dinner—catfish her boy had caught that afternoon, green beans and biscuits. Willie June hovered in the kitchen, trying to be helpful. She set out forks and paper napkins. She filled cups with water and set them carefully on the table.

Mother Franklin said, "Got yourself a good girl, Gus."

"Don't know what I'd do without my Willie June," Gussie said.

"And me too, Mama. Me too!" Gaynelle wanted part of that praise.

"Go on over and fetch Gwen. Miz Roberts made enough to feed her, too," Gussie said, shooing Gaynelle out the back door.

"You carryin' a heavy burden with so many mouths to feed," Mother Franklin said.

"Lord, he provide."

"You gotta be bone tired, Gussie Munroe."

A few minutes later Gaynelle pulled Gwen into the kitchen. She let go of Gwen's hand only long enough for her to get settled in a chair and then she scrambled up into the young woman's lap. She smoothed Gwen's long hair and rubbed her shoulders. Gwen laughed. "Child, what you doin', pettin' me like some pussy cat?"

"You the queen, Gwen. You the queen." Gaynelle said. "When the baby gets here you gone let me tend him?"

"Maybe she'll let you change diapers," Gussie said.

Gwen laughed again and settled Gaynelle in her own chair.

Gussie and Willie June carried plates of food to the table.

"Where you stay when you not at praying camp?" Gwen asked.

"I be at Savannah," Mother Franklin told her. "Sometimes. Out the beach. It nice. Out there." Partial sentences lurched from between her lips as if some of her words got swallowed along with a mouthful of food.

"Mama, when can we go to the beach?" Gaynelle asked. "Aunt Nethra and them go every year."

Tyrell was crumbling his biscuit, rolling it around on the table, watching it break into a thousand tiny bits. "I wanna go the beach."

"You too little, Tyrell," Gwen said, reached over the table to tickle him. "The fish'd eat you for dinner."

"I ain't little no more, Mama," Gaynelle said. "So when c'n I go?"

Mother Franklin chewed her fish, unaware; then finally swallowing, she said, "It is the glory of God to conceal things, but the glory of kings is to search things out." She looked across the table. "Now Gus, why these girls ain't never been to the beach?"

"Can't afford no foolishness like that," Gussie mumbled.

Miz Roberts hadn't brought cake, the fish was dry, her green beans tasted mostly of vinegar; and Lord, her biscuits were hard as rocks.

That night after dinner, the children went to bed in Gussie's room. The boys fell asleep without too much bother. Willie June, too. But not Gaynelle. "It's too dark in here, Mama." Gaynelle sounded tearful. "Why can't we put a light on?"

"Child, we got to turn them lights off; all the lights. Don't we have to be saving on that Duke Power bill?"

"But Mama, there's a boogie man at the window. He's gone get me, Mama. I know it."

"Ain't no boogie man out there, Gaynelle."

Gaynelle called again to her mother. "Why ain't you afraid, Mama? Of the dark?"

"Lord child, I only be afraid of what shows itself in the daylight." Gussie sat on the edge of the bed and tried to explain how the dark can be your friend. "Dark ain't nothing to fear. If you try," Gussie whispered, "you can even turn off the lights inside your head. Shut out all the lights and get you some sound sleep."

Gaynelle screwed her eyes shut, then opened them again. "'At's too scary, Mama. I want it bright and shiny in my head. I don't wanna be in the dark."

"You ain't never gone get no rest that way."

"Can't nobody snatch me away if everything's all lit up." Gaynelle said.

"Shut your eyes, baby girl. Turn them lights off and get you some sleep."

Gaynelle whimpered in the dark. Tyrell tossed and turned. Willie June snored softly.

Gussie closed her eyes. She could imagine herself a nice dark room. She could make it be cool and quiet there if she pushed the door tight against the jamb, leaned all her weight against it. Gaynelle and Willie June and the boys, nothing but noise all day. But not here. No. Not even

Gussie was crying in here.

Here in this room, it was quiet. *No laundry, no iron. No spitting, hissing worry. No nasty. No dirty. No bad.*

Just quiet.

Just dark.

No more old men in here. Just the babies. Oh, no babies, neither. Don't want me no more babies.

Just dark.

No mens.

No babies.

No more.

Just quiet.

Please, Jesus, just the dark. Don't need no light. Don't need no light to lead me nowhere.

While Gussie could keep it dark, it was harder to keep it quiet. She heard things just like the blind old man she tended to. That old man, couldn't see a thing, but he could hear. Sharp as a tack.

Gussie heard mice gnawing at boxes. At the mattress. At her feet. She heard people telling her things. Secrets.

Don't tell no one.

Brother Pomeroy, *No need to be spreading this about, Gussie. This just between us. Give me some love, woman.*

And Gwen, *Them girls. Them girls getting so big, Gussie. How you gone feed all these mouths? Ain't even room for all of you.*

And Mother Franklin, *I done speak to the Lord, my children, and the Lord he say to me lose your burdens. Drop them off your backs. Lay them down, children.*

And who be the biggest burdens of them all?

Lay them down, sister, said Mother Franklin. *Lay them down at the altar.*

Miz Jenkins brought dinner the second night, greens with pot liquor and big, juicy hunks of smoked pork. No crumbly biscuits neither, but a whole skillet of cornbread, bright yellow and buttery.

Gussie spooned collards out of the pot and placed squares of cornbread onto plates that felt as if they weighed one hundred pounds. It was all she could do to carry them to the table. Lord, but she was tired. Gaynelle had kept her up most of the night, and all day the old man had been as fussy as her baby Jo-Jo. Must be the heat. It was so hot in the kitchen the only one eating with any appetite was Mother Franklin.

"Air sure is heavy tonight," Gussie said and pulled her hair away from her forehead, raked her fingers through it. "Maybe later we get some rain."

"Mama," Tyrell pulled on his mother's sleeve. "Willie June just pinched me."

Gussie said, "Willie June, why'n't you run get those things off the line 'fore it rains."

Willie June went out the back door, letting the screen slap loudly behind her.

Gaynelle tried to sit on Gwen's lap but had to settle for leaning against her in the cramped space between the table and the wall. "This be nice," Gaynelle said smoothing Gwen's shirt across her back.

"Gaynelle, stop fussing at Gwen," Gussie said.

"I ain't fussin'," Gaynelle said.

"Y'all's done with supper now. Take the boys in the front room. Go on now." Gussie fanned her face with her hand. "What you have more of, Mother Franklin?"

"I'll let this go," she said, handing her plate to Gussie, "to get me more cornbread if you have it."

"It this hot where you stay?" Gwen asked.

"Sometimes you c'n catch the wind. Out there. That wind'll lift you up, make you feel 'most like heaven."

Gussie cut two pieces of cornbread and placed them side by side on a fresh plate.

Mother Franklin braced her hands on the ruined table and stood, a mammoth figure in purple satin pleats. "I have shown you all things, how that so labouring ye ought to support the weak, and to remember the words of the Lord Jesus, how he said, 'It is more blessed to give than to receive.'"

Gussie set the golden squares of cornbread at the head of the table. Mother Franklin handed her an envelope, crumpled and bulky.

"But how we poor sinners suffer," the old woman said. "Cry and wail son of man. Put your burdens down, sinners. Put your burdens down."

"Amen, sister," Gwen said.

"Amen," said Mother Franklin.

Gussie tucked the envelope under her plate; a mess of greens still sat there, the broth soaking her cornbread. "Too hot to eat," she said and leaned back against her chair.

Tomorrow she'd go on up to the Top Inn, order herself a whole chicken box and suck the meat right off the bones.

ACKNOWLEDGEMENTS

Thank you, Steve Matanle for befriending Marann early on, for forcing me to choose present over past and for knowing where every errant comma belongs.

Thank you, Naná Howton for many mornings spent with the Nigerian sisters of Kefa, and for instant and enduring friendship. This is our year.

And Barbara Blaker Krumdieck, who knows how things in Augusta really roll, thank you for good times spent over (probably too many) glasses of Prosecco.

Thank you, Mizz M, to whom I owe my very name and whose annual gift of blank pages (and chocolate with mint) fueled these stories and more.

And Maggie Smith and Earthelle Latta for opening worlds otherwise closed to me—thank you.

ABOUT THE AUTHOR

Avery Caswell, a native of Chicago, eventually found her true home in North Carolina. She is fascinated by the moon, drives far too fast and wishes she could remember at least one good joke. (averycaswell.com)

ABOUT THE TYPE

The text of *MotherLoad* is set in Goudy Old Style, a classic old-style serif typeface originally created by Frederic W. Goudy for American Type Founders (ATF) in 1915. Some of this font's attributes—most notably the gently curved, rounded serifs of certain glyphs—evoke a Venetian influence. Goudy sold the design to ATF for $1500 and received no royalties even though the face was an instant best seller.

Goudy kept books for a Chicago Realtor and did not begin designing type until age 40. During the next 36 years, he cut 113 fonts of type, creating more usable faces than did the seven greatest inventors of type and books —from Gutenberg to Garamond.

31901056465596